Other books by Howard Schwartz and Barbara Rush

The Diamond Tree: Jewish Tales from Around the World
Pictures in full color by Uri Shulevitz

The Sabbath Lion: A Jewish Folktale from Algeria
Pictures in full color by Stephen Fieser

Books edited by Howard Schwartz

Elijah's Violin & Other Jewish Fairy Tales

Miriam's Tambourine: Jewish Folktales from Around the World

Lilith's Cave: Jewish Tales of the Supernatural

Gabriel's Palace: Jewish Mystical Tales

Books edited by Barbara Rush

Great Teachers of Israel

The Jews of Kurdistan

Seventy and One Tales for the Jewish Year: Folktales for the Festivals

The Book of Jewish Women's Tales

THE
WONDER
CHILD

& Other Jewish Fairy Tales

SELECTED AND RETOLD

BY HOWARD SCHWARTZ

AND BARBARA RUSH

ILLUSTRATED BY STEPHEN FIESER

HARPERCOLLINS*PUBLISHERS*

Some of these stories have been previously published in *Cricket* and *The Sagarin Review*.

The Wonder Child & Other Jewish Fairy Tales
Text copyright © 1992, 1993, 1994, 1995, 1996 by Howard Schwartz and Barbara Rush
Illustrations copyright © 1996 by Stephen Fieser
Library of Congress Cataloging-in-Publication Data
Schwartz, Howard, 1945–
    The wonder child & other Jewish fairy tales / selected and retold by Howard Schwartz and Barbara Rush ; illustrated by Stephen Fieser.
        p.   cm.
    Summary: An illustrated collection of traditional Jewish tales from various countries.
    ISBN 0-06-023517-9. — ISBN 0-06-023518-7 (lib bdg.)
    1. Fairy tales.   2. Jews—Folklore.   [1. Fairy tales.   2. Jews—Folklore.   3. Folklore.]
I. Rush, Barbara.   II. Fieser, Stephen, ill.   III. Title.   IV. Title: Wonder child & other Jewish fairy tales.
PZ8.S31285Wo   1996   94-32542
398.2'089'924—dc20   CIP
                                                                                                                  AC

Typography by Al Cetta
1 2 3 4 5 6 7 8 9 10
❖
First Edition

CONTENTS

INTRODUCTION

For centuries, Jewish parents and grandparents have sat around the fireplace at night, sharing tales with their children—the very same stories they were told when they were young. Sometimes these stories resemble fairy tales from around the world, and sometimes they are uniquely Jewish.

Each of these stories draws on well-known fairy tale figures, such as kings and queens, princes and princesses, and every kind of supernatural being, but colors them according to the Jewish time and place from which they emerged. And since the Jews are a wandering people, these stories come from every corner of the earth.

In "The Wonder Child," a Jewish tale from Egypt, there are hints of both "Snow White" and "Sleeping Beauty." But here it is a lovely Jewish girl who sleeps night and day after an evil queen tries to kill her. In "The Forest Witch," from Eastern Europe, the witch is every bit as demanding as the imp in "Rumpelstiltskin," but she meets her match in a Jewish mother who is determined to save not only her child, but her husband as well.

So, too, are there classic Jewish versions of tales about giants, werewolves, demons, and impossible quests, represented here by "The Tailors and the Giant," "The Rabbi Who Became a Werewolf," "The Black Cat," and "The Long Hair of the Princess." These stories come from Eastern Europe and the Middle East.

Tales that are uniquely Jewish include "The Peddler and the Sprite," in which a Jewish imp loves to play tricks on people, and "The Purim Dybbuk," in which a boy must be saved from the cranky spirit that has possessed him. In each of these stories it takes a clever Jewish hero to outwit these sneaky creatures.

Some of the best examples of Jewish fairy tales are collected here—stories that have survived for centuries, passed on from one generation to the next. Now it is your turn to receive them.

THE WONDER CHILD

Long ago, there lived a rabbi and his wife who had no children. They prayed every day for a child of their own, but their prayers were never answered.

Now it is said that the sky opens at midnight on the night of Shavuoth, and any prayers or wishes made at that time come true. So one Shavuoth the rabbi and his wife decided to stay awake, so that their prayers would be certain to reach God's ears.

To their amazement, at midnight the sky parted like the waters of the Red Sea, and for one instant the world was filled with the glory of heaven. And in that instant both the rabbi and his

wife wished for a child. That night the rabbi's wife dreamed of a wonder child, a girl who would be born to them clutching a precious jewel. In the dream the rabbi's wife was told that the child must keep the jewel with her at all times, for her soul was inside it. And if she ever lost that jewel, she would fall into a deep sleep from which she would not awaken until the jewel was returned.

The next morning, the rabbi's wife told her husband the dream, and he was much amazed. And, indeed, things occurred exactly as foretold, and nine months later a beautiful baby girl was born. In her right hand she clutched a precious jewel, which seemed to glow with a light of its own. The rabbi and his wife named their daughter Kohava, which means "star," and the rabbi set the jewel in a necklace for her to wear around her neck.

One day, when Kohava was only three years old, she picked up her mother's flute. She had never played a flute before, but the moment she put it to her lips, beautiful melodies poured forth. Not only could she play any musical instrument, but at a very early age, she taught herself to paint lovely pictures, to write the letters of the alphabet, and to read books. Her favorites were the books on her father's shelves that told stories of the ancient days when Abraham and Moses walked in the world.

As the years passed, Kohava grew into a beautiful girl. Her lustrous black hair shone in the sunlight. Her dark eyes sparkled like the dazzling jewel she wore around her neck. Her skin was as smooth as the outside of a peach, and her smile brought happiness to everyone who met her.

Now the rabbi and his wife realized that their daughter was truly a wonder child, as the dream had promised, and they gave thanks to God. But in their hearts was the fear that someday she might be separated from her necklace and lose her soul. That is why the rabbi and his wife watched carefully over Kohava and rarely let her leave home.

One day the rabbi and his wife learned that the queen was going to visit the bathhouse that very day and that she had invited all the women of the village to come there. Kohava asked her mother if she, too, could go, for she had never seen the queen. At first her mother was afraid, but at last she agreed to let her go.

When the two arrived at the bathhouse, the women looked at Kohava in amazement. "Where did she come from? Why, she is more beautiful than the queen!" they exclaimed.

When the queen heard this, she grew angry. "Who is this girl?" she asked her servants. They replied that Kohava was a Jewish girl of great beauty and that it was said that she could play any musical instrument set before her.

The queen demanded to see Kohava for herself. And when she realized that the girl's beauty did indeed outshine her own, she was filled with jealousy, and with the sudden fear that her son, the prince, might see Kohava and fall in love with her. And that would be a terrible thing, for she wanted the prince to marry a princess, not a poor Jewish girl.

The queen had one of her servants bring forth a flute and commanded the girl to play it. At once Kohava played a melody so beautiful that it brought tears to everyone's eyes. Everyone's,

that is, except the queen's. Then the queen commanded that the girl play a violin, and after that a harp. And from every instrument that Kohava touched, beautiful melodies poured forth. When the queen saw that Kohava truly had a great talent, she ordered: "This girl must return with me at once to my palace to serve as one of my royal musicians."

The rabbi's wife was heartsick at the thought of Kohava's going off to live in the palace, yet she knew that they must obey the queen. But before Kohava left, her mother took her aside and whispered that she should never, ever take off her necklace, nor should she tell anyone that it held her soul. Then the mother and daughter kissed good-bye, and Kohava rode off in the royal carriage with the queen.

Now the queen had no intention of letting Kohava be a musician, for in that way her son, the prince, might see her. Alas, as soon as they reached the palace, she shut Kohava in the dungeon and ordered that she be left to starve.

So it was that the confused girl found herself imprisoned and frightened for her very life. She would have died of hunger had not the prison guard, overwhelmed by her beauty and gentleness, brought her food in secret. In her dark cell, Kohava wept for her mother and father, and prayed to be saved from the evil queen.

One day the queen went down to the dungeon to see for herself if Kohava was still alive. As she walked into the dark cell, she was surprised to see a glowing light. When she looked closer, she realized that the light was coming from the jewel Kohava wore around her neck, and that the girl was, indeed, still alive.

"Give me that necklace!" the queen demanded. "I want it for myself." Kohava was terrified, for she remembered her mother's warning. But the queen, not waiting for Kohava to obey, pulled it off herself. And the moment she did, Kohava sank into a deep sleep.

The queen was delighted, for she thought that the girl was dead. "Ah, I'm rid of her for good," she cried. Then she ordered the prison guard to bury Kohava far away from the palace where no one could ever find her. But when the guard reached the woods far away from the palace, he saw that Kohava was still breathing, and he realized that she was only asleep. So he brought her to a hut he knew of in the forest, and left her there. Day after day, Kohava slept a long, dreamless sleep, and no one except the guard knew she was there.

One afternoon, when the prince was out riding in the woods far away from the palace, he saw that very hut and decided to stop and rest there. When the prince entered, he was astonished to find a sleeping girl, and he lost his heart to her the moment he saw her. The prince wanted to tell her of his love, but when he realized that she would not wake up, he was very sad. So the prince put a guard outside the hut to protect the sleeping beauty. Every day he came to visit her, and every day he shed tears because she would not awaken.

As the days passed, the queen noticed the sadness of her son, and one day she asked him what was wrong. He told his mother that he was in love with a beautiful young girl.

"Is she a princess?" asked the queen.

"Surely," said the prince, "she is a princess."

"In that case," said the queen, "would you like to give her a gift to show your love?"

"Oh, yes," said the prince, "I would like that very much."

"Then I know just the gift for a beautiful princess," replied the queen. "It is something very special." And she brought forth the jewel that she had taken from Kohava. The prince took the necklace to the sleeping girl at once, and the moment he put it around her neck, she woke up.

"Who are you?" asked Kohava as she looked around the small hut. "And where am I?"

The prince told Kohava how he had found her and how she had awakened at the very moment he placed the necklace around her neck.

Kohava looked at the jewel and remembered how the queen had snatched it from her. "Where did you get this?" she asked.

And so she learned that the one who had saved her was none other than the queen's son. And when the prince learned of his mother's evil deed, he realized that Kohava's life was in danger. He decided to leave the girl in the hut while he hurried back to the palace.

When he arrived, he went straight to the queen. "Mother, I have great news," he said. "I'd like to get married."

"I can see how much you love this princess," said the queen. "I will give orders for the wedding preparations to begin at once!"

Every servant worked night and day. The cooks prepared a magnificent feast, the gardeners cut huge bouquets of roses, and the maids polished the silver goblets until they shone. By the seventh day everything was ready. All the people of the kingdom

came. They gathered at the palace and whispered to one another, "Who is the bride?" For not even the queen had seen her. But when the bride arrived, she was wearing seven veils, and no one could tell who she was.

Among the thousands of guests were the rabbi and his wife, who had come hoping they might see their daughter, Kohava, from whom they had not heard since the day the queen had brought her to the palace.

At last the wedding vows were spoken, and the guests waited breathlessly as the prince lifted the veils, one by one. And as he lifted the seventh veil, everyone gasped at Kohava's great beauty. Everyone, that is, except the rabbi and his wife, who could not believe their eyes, and the queen, who thought that she was seeing a ghost. Screaming with terror, she ran from the palace as fast as she could—and never was seen again.

So it was that the prince and his new bride became the rulers of the kingdom, and Kohava was reunited with her father and mother. At the palace Kohava continued to play music and make people happy with her songs. And the love that Kohava and the prince had for each other grew deeper over the years, and they lived happily ever after.

EGYPT: ORAL TRADITION

THE LONG HAIR
OF THE PRINCESS

Once upon a time there was a king who had only one daughter, and everyone who saw her agreed that she was the most beautiful girl in all the world. Her skin was soft, and her raven-black hair was as fine as silk, and it was longer and shinier than that of any other maiden in the kingdom. But the princess was not only beautiful, she was also kind to every living creature. Her heart was full of singing, and everyone who saw her loved her for her goodness and her beauty.

In that same kingdom was a demon who lived in a palace at the bottom of the sea. This demon slept all year long—except on his

birthday, when he would awaken and go forth to see the world.

Now it happened that the demon left his underwater palace on his birthday and spied the princess walking beside the sea, tossing bread crumbs to the sea gulls. Right then the demon decided he wanted her for himself. So he grabbed her by her long black hair and dragged her to his palace beneath the sea.

The demon led the princess to his bedroom, and just before it was time for him to fall asleep again, he grasped her long hair and said, "Know that I sleep all but one day of each year. But now that you are mine, you must stay here with me. I will hold your hair in my hand, and if you ever try to escape, I will awaken just long enough to kill you and anyone else who tries to take you from me!" And with those frightening words, the demon went back to sleep for another year, the long hair of the princess clasped tightly in his hand.

Meanwhile, the king at the royal palace moaned and cried, "Where is my daughter? Where can she be?" He knew only that the beautiful princess was missing, but search as he might, he could find no trace of her in all the kingdom.

Then the king called forth his guards. "Search carefully," he ordered, "for if, within three days, you have not learned what has happened to my daughter, your lives will be lost!"

So the guards searched everywhere for some sign of the lost princess: between the leaves in the forest, between the blades of grass, between the grains of sand. And then, at the edge of the shore, they found one long, black hair as fine as silk. It was, of course, a hair of the princess, which had come loose when the demon had pulled her hair.

The guards showed that hair to an old woman who lived nearby and discovered that she herself had seen the terrible kidnapping. Indeed, the people of that place all knew about the dangerous demon, and had learned long ago to hide in their houses on the demon's birthday and to stay out of his way.

That is how the king learned that his beautiful daughter had been taken to the palace of the demon who lived beneath the sea. "How can I get my daughter back from the palace of the demon?" cried the worried king. "Many are those who have heard of the demon's palace, but who has the power to travel beneath the sea to reach it?"

And what did the king do then? Why, he sent messengers to every corner of the kingdom, to every city and every village, to every mountain and every valley, to every cottage and every house: "Come one and all! Let it be known that to whoever can rescue the princess from the demon who lives in the palace beneath the sea, the king will give half his kingdom—and the hand of the princess in marriage."

Soon many young men arrived from all corners of the kingdom to try their luck. Each one was strong and handsome and clever, and each tried to dive beneath the sea, or build a tunnel to the demon's palace, so that the princess might be freed. But try as they might, not one could reach the palace of the evil demon.

At last seven young men came to the palace and offered to save the princess. For they said among themselves: "If one man cannot accomplish this alone, perhaps we will succeed by working together." Who were they? One was a carpenter; one was a

painter; one was a blacksmith; one was a sailor; one was a wizard; one was a thief; and one was a hunter.

And what did they do? The carpenter built a fine boat, and the painter sealed and painted it, so that it was safe from rough seas. The blacksmith made weapons, fine spears and arrows, to protect the men from the anger of the demon. Then the sailor rigged the sails, so that all seven could set forth on their journey. And then the wizard pronounced a magic spell, and at once the boat went down through the water and made its way straight to the palace beneath the sea. Once there, the wizard took out a crystal ball, and by looking into it, he was able to find the very room in which the demon slept. And there too he saw the princess, seated near the sleeping demon, her long black hair clutched in his hand!

So the young men hurried to that room, and the thief threw a long rope in through the window, and the princess, who was very happy to see them, quickly tied one end of it around herself. But when the young men began to pull her out through the open window, the sleeping demon felt the princess's hair slipping slowly through his fingers. He awoke, furious indeed. "Oh, you think you can take the princess from me, do you?" he shouted, jumping up. And he was just about to cast a spell, turning all the young men into little fish, when the hunter threw a spear straight into the demon's heart, and the demon fell down dead!

Quickly the seven men led the princess to the boat and took her back to her earthly home. How happy her father was to see her! A party was held, and everyone in the kingdom joined in the celebration. Platters were heaped high with sweet cakes of wheat

and honey. Dancers in colorful costumes entertained the guests, while women sang and clapped their hands in songs of joy.

When the time came to reward the rescuers, each young man came forward to claim the fortune and the hand of the princess in marriage. But to which young man should the king give half his kingdom? Which young man deserved to marry his daughter?

Was it the carpenter? After all, he had built the boat. Was it the painter? After all, he had sealed and painted it to make it safe. Was it the blacksmith? After all, he had made the weapons. Was it the sailor? After all, he had rigged the sails. Was it the wizard? After all, he had made the boat dive beneath the sea. Was it the thief? After all, he had thrown the rope. Or was it the hunter? After all, his perfect aim had killed the demon.

The king did not know which one deserved the hand of his daughter, so he turned to the princess and said, "My daughter, all these brave young men are worthy of your hand in marriage, but only *you* know which one you wish to wed, and only *you* shall decide. Which of the seven did the most to rescue you?"

The princess answered, "You are right, Father. I owe a great debt to all seven men, and surely all deserve to share in my good fortune. But I can wed only one. Who shall it be?"

The princess hesitated. She thought for a long time. The king and all the royal court leaned forward to hear her words.

At last the princess spoke: "I choose . . . the wizard, for without his magic I would still be in the demon's palace beneath the sea. After all, many carpenters can build boats, many painters can paint boats, many blacksmiths can make weapons, many sailors can rig sails, many thieves can toss ropes, and many hunters can

throw spears—but only the most remarkable wizard can make a boat dive safely to the bottom of the sea. Without his magic, none of the young men would have reached the demon's palace, nor would they have found the demon's room."

Then all the court applauded the princess and the young man she had chosen to wed. For everyone, including the king, believed that she had made a wise choice. The royal wedding was arranged. The grandest people in all the kingdom were invited to attend, and, of course, the other six brave young men were invited as well.

Now it so happened that just before the wedding, when the princess and the wizard were walking through the garden, they came upon six delicate roses that had appeared as if from nowhere.

"That's strange," said the princess. "I never noticed these roses before."

And then the wizard, whose powers were truly remarkable, said a few magic words, and all at once the roses vanished. In their place stood six beautiful princesses, one for each of the other six brave men. And so it was that all seven of the beautiful princesses and all seven of the young men were wed at the same time, and every single one of them lived happily ever after.

LIBYA: ORAL TRADITION

THE BLACK CAT

The story is still told to this day in the land of Morocco about the girl Zipporah and the black cat. Zipporah lived with her grandmother and helped take care of their animals. She loved her grandmother's goat and cow and chickens, and she treated them like her own pets.

But most of all, Zipporah loved the black cat that often wandered near their house. It drank the milk Zipporah gave it and rubbed against her legs.

But her grandmother warned her to stay away from it. "Black cats are bad luck," she said.

How could this be? Zipporah had never known a nicer cat, but she didn't want to upset her grandmother. So Zipporah played with the cat only when she was out in the fields with the goat.

Now Zipporah's grandmother was a midwife. She helped other women when they gave birth, for there were no doctors in their small village. She had helped bring a great many children into the world, and everyone thought she was very wise.

At night Grandmother would tell Zipporah many stories: sometimes tales of fairy princesses, and sometimes spooky tales about demons and spirits and all kinds of strange beings. Zipporah loved the tales and wondered if they were true, but she hoped she would never, ever see such creatures herself.

There were many caves near the village where Zipporah and her grandmother lived. Zipporah's grandmother often warned her to stay away from them. "Snakes and other wild animals live there," she said. "People even say that demons live there as well."

One day when Zipporah took the goat out to graze, it ran away. She chased it all afternoon and all evening until the goat disappeared into a cave. Zipporah remembered her grandmother's warning and did not go inside the cave. But when she looked around, she realized that she was lost. And even worse, it was growing dark.

Now Zipporah was a very brave girl, but she had never been lost at night before. She heard strange sounds and was afraid. And when something brushed against her leg, she was so frightened that she cried out. But then she heard a familiar meowing in the dark—it was her friend the black cat.

Over and over the cat rubbed against her. It meowed and took a few steps away, until Zipporah realized that the cat was trying to lead her home. So Zipporah took hold of the cat's tail and let it lead her. And the goat? It came trotting out of the cave and followed right behind.

Imagine how happy Zipporah was when she saw the flame of her grandmother's lamp burning in the window of their house. Zipporah's grandmother hugged and kissed her. "Zipporah, I was so worried that I was just about to set out with a torch to find you," she said.

But then Grandmother saw the eyes of the black cat gleaming in the darkness outside the door, and she rushed to get her broom.

"Oh, don't chase it away, Grandmother," Zipporah cried. "That cat led me home!"

Well, what could Grandmother do? The cat had saved her beloved Zipporah, so she allowed it to stay near the house.

Zipporah and the cat continued to play together, and soon she began to notice that the black cat was growing larger and larger every day, and she guessed it would soon have kittens. Zipporah could hardly wait to play with them. But then one day the black cat disappeared.

Zipporah didn't see the cat for a week, even though she searched everywhere, near the house and in the fields. She really missed her friend. Where could it have gone? Then one morning, while walking the goat, she thought she saw her beloved cat walking her way. But when the cat came closer, she saw that it was a different black cat, much larger, with a white marking like a crown on its forehead.

When the cat came closer still, it rubbed against Zipporah's legs and meowed, and seemed to want to lead her somewhere. Zipporah was surprised, but at last she followed the black cat. She tugged at the rope of the goat so it would come too. "Will this cat lead me to my lost black cat?" she wondered.

The large cat led Zipporah to the caves. But when the cat saw that she did not want to go inside, it went in alone. And a minute later the cat came out, carrying something in its mouth. And what did it drop at Zipporah's feet? A shiny piece of gold.

Now Zipporah's grandmother was very poor, and Zipporah knew that one piece of gold could buy food for them for a whole year. What if there were more gold pieces inside the cave? And so, even though she was still afraid, Zipporah picked up the piece of gold, tied the goat to a nearby tree, and went into the cave after all. But when she stepped inside, she did not find herself in a place that was dark and scary. No! Instead, the cave was as beautiful as a palace. Zipporah looked around for the cat, but it had disappeared. Just then she heard a gentle voice call her name from the next room: "Zipporah . . . Zipporah!"

Zipporah might have been frightened to find someone else in that cave, but the voice sounded like one she had heard before, so Zipporah plucked up her courage and walked through the doorway.

There she saw a beautiful woman, with long, black hair, sitting up in bed. The woman was pregnant, and Zipporah could tell that it wouldn't be long before she gave birth, for she had seen many pregnant women who had come to her grandmother.

"Hello, Zipporah," said the woman. "Do you know me?"

"No," said Zipporah. "Who are you?"

"I am the black cat that saved you when you were lost in the dark," the woman replied. "The cat to whom you are so kind, the cat that is about to give birth."

Zipporah could hardly believe her ears. But she knew it must be true. How else could the woman know her name and how she had gotten lost?

"I am not human like you," said the woman. "I live in the Kingdom of Demons. But when I leave that kingdom, I take the shape of a black cat."

"Does that mean that you are a demon?" asked Zipporah in a frightened voice.

"Yes," the woman replied, "but you need not be afraid, for I am a good demon. Indeed, I sent my husband to bring you here because I need your help."

"Your husband?" asked Zipporah in amazement.

"Yes," said a voice behind her. And when Zipporah turned around, she saw a tall, kind-looking man with black hair. And around his neck he wore a medallion decorated with a crown. And it looked just like the white marking on the head of the black cat that had led her there!

"You must be the other cat!" said Zipporah.

"Yes," said the man. "And we thank you for coming here."

"But what do you want from me?" Zipporah asked.

"We need you to go to your grandmother," said the man, "and ask her to come back here to help deliver the child. We know that she is afraid of demons, but now you can explain to her that

your friend the black cat needs her help. Take the piece of gold with you, so she will believe you."

Now Zipporah understood. So she took the gold and left. And as soon as she untied the goat, the large black cat with the white crown reappeared and led them all the way home.

As soon as Zipporah saw her grandmother, she told her what had happened and showed her the piece of gold. Her grandmother gasped. "Yes, I will come at once," she said. "I will be happy to help the cat that helped you."

As soon as they left the house, Zipporah and her grandmother saw that the male cat was waiting to lead them both to the cave. There Zipporah's grandmother entered the room just in time to help with the birth.

Before long two crying babies could be heard, for the mother demon had given birth to twins. Much to Zipporah's surprise, they looked like human babies in every way, and they both had the black hair of their mother and father.

"Thank you for coming to help us," said the father demon. "I wish to give you a reward. Ask for anything you want and it shall be yours."

"Oh no," answered Grandmother, "I do not want anything. Just doing a good deed is my reward."

"But you must take something," said the cat, and he handed her a bag filled with garlic. Amazed at all that had happened that day, Grandmother took the bag, and she and Zipporah carried it all the way home.

Then, just as they reached their door, the bag of garlic suddenly felt heavy, so heavy that Grandmother almost dropped it.

She looked inside, and what did she see? All that garlic had turned to gold!

So it was that Zipporah and her grandmother never had to worry about being poor again, and they were very generous to one and all. But they still lived in the same house and kept their chickens and goat and cow, and Zipporah loved them all. Best of all she loved the black cat and its two black kittens that often came to visit and play. And, of course, they were always welcome in the house of Zipporah and her grandmother.

MOROCCO: ORAL TRADITION

THE FOREST WITCH

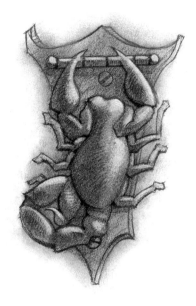

The rabbi's son and the son of the shammes were the best of friends. They shared their toys, their games, and even their secrets. One day when the two boys were passing through the woods, they decided to play a game of hide and seek. The son of the shammes went to hide, while his friend set out to find him.

As he searched near a giant tree, the rabbi's son saw a strange sight. There, sticking out from the tree, was a small hand, one finger of which pointed straight ahead, as if pointing the way. The rabbi's son thought it was the hand of his friend,

so he decided to play a joke on him. Taking off his own ring and placing it on the pointing finger, he said aloud, "With this ring you are wed to me." Then he repeated the vow two more times, as people do at weddings.

But as he watched, the finger slipped back into the tree, and from inside the hollow trunk stepped a frightfully ugly woman. A cold chill went down the boy's back. Her face was as white as chalk, her eyes glowed like burning coals, and her long, black hair hung below her waist. She said nothing, but her smile was evil.

The boy knew at once that this woman was none other than the forest witch, about whom he had heard his father speak. It was said that she had magic powers over all the animals in the forest and that she could turn herself into any forest creature. The boy was so frightened that he froze on the spot, but then he came to his senses and ran as quickly as he could through the woods, calling out to his friend to come with him. And when the friend heard the fear in his voice, he too dashed out of the forest. Never once did they look back. And, at last, they came safely home.

Many years passed. The rabbi's son grew up and forgot about the frightful woman. The time came for him to be married. His father chose a lovely bride for him from a most distinguished family, and the wedding ceremony was celebrated by all the people of the town.

But when the wedding was over and the bride and groom were left by themselves, a frightful woman appeared in front of them, blocking their path. She was pale of face, with long, black

hair, and she was pointing one of her bony fingers at them. The groom knew at once that she was the same witch he had met years before in the woods.

The witch spoke in a rasping voice. "You are *my* husband, and I have come to claim you! How did you ever think you could wed another?"

The bride stood in disbelief. "What is she talking about?" she asked her husband. "Surely she lies!"

But before the startled groom could open his mouth to reply, the strange woman spoke again: "Like it or not, my words are true." And with that she raised her pointing finger, which held the ring of the rabbi's son. The groom recognized his ring at once and, unable to speak, stood frozen with his mouth open.

"You recited the wedding vow three times," said the witch. "Therefore, according to the law, you are *my* husband."

The bride turned to her husband. "Say it isn't true!" she begged, but the groom could only nod his head sadly, in agreement with the witch. She, in turn, put her long bony arm around the groom, as if to lead him away.

"Wait!" cried the wife. "Let us make a bargain. Give me a chance to get my husband back!"

The witch stopped. Her dark eyes were full of fire. She loved nothing better than making bargains, for she was certain that she would win. After all, weren't her powers greater than those of a foolish bride?

"Very well," she hissed. "I will release him from his vow. But when you have a son and he reaches the age of manhood, I will come to claim him. He shall be mine."

The bride thought, "Oh, that day is surely far away. Between now and then, I'll find a way to change the witch's mind." And so she agreed.

Some years passed. The young couple did, indeed, have a son who grew up to be clever and handsome. When the boy was thirteen years old, he became a Bar Mitzvah, and his proud parents were filled with joy.

But that very night, as the young man slept, the witch appeared before the boy's mother. "Do you remember your promise?" she hissed. "Your son has grown to be a man. Now I have come to claim him."

The woman gasped. She had not forgotten the bargain she had made, but she had not expected the witch so soon. What could she do?

"Please," she begged, "give me another chance. Ask for anything and I will give it to you, but don't take my son!"

The witch was about to snatch the boy, but suddenly her eyes began to glow. Here was her chance to win another bargain, and there was nothing she loved better than bargaining. So she replied, "Very well, my dear, I will give you three days to find out where I live. If you do, I will release you from your promise. But if by midnight on the third day you have not found my home, I will take your son and your husband. They will come in handy as slaves!"

And so saying, she hopped out the window, screeching, and as she jumped down, she called out, "Remember, you have only three days left!"

The woman sat stunned. What could she do? How could she

stop the witch? It was well known that the forest witch could turn herself into any creature in the forest: a bird, a snake, a bear. Why, she could hide in any tree, in any cave, under any rock. How could anyone find her?

But the woman had to try, so she set out to search the forest. She looked in caves, and behind trees, and under rocks, but she could find no sign of the witch. She asked an old woodcutter she met in the forest, and an old woman who lived in a small hut nearby, and villagers who were gathering flowers in the forest, but no one could tell her where the witch lived.

Two days passed. The woman became desperate.

At last, on the afternoon of the third day, while the woman was walking in a clearing in the forest, a deer dashed past her. She caught only a quick glance at the animal, but in that one glance she saw that the deer's face was pale, and its eyes glowed in a way that was strangely familiar.

At that instant the woman knew that the deer was none other than the forest witch. She ran in the direction of the deer, just in time to see the deer turn itself into a squirrel. And that squirrel also had eyes exactly like the eyes of the witch.

The squirrel dashed ahead until it came to a well, and there it turned into a big bullfrog and jumped into the well. The woman ran to the well just as fast as she could. And when she looked down, she saw the frog climb into an opening near the bottom of the well. So she quickly climbed into the bucket and lowered herself down the well after it.

When the woman reached the place where she had seen the frog, she found that there was a door there, and on it was an iron

knocker in the shape of a scorpion. And when she put her ear against the door, she heard a voice coming from inside. It was the hissing voice of the forest witch. "Oh, that silly woman! She'll never find me. How will she ever know that I live behind a door at the bottom of a well? Ha! Tomorrow her son and her husband will both be mine."

The woman was ever so happy to hear this. That was all she needed to know. She waited quietly in the bucket until the witch fell asleep and she could hear her snoring. Then she pulled off the iron knocker shaped like a scorpion and dropped it into a leather pouch. She quickly raised the bucket to the top of the well and ran home.

At midnight the witch arrived. She sneered at the woman. "There'll be no more bargaining, my dear. Admit that you lost! Tell your son and your husband to follow me."

"Not so fast!" said the woman. "How do you know that I didn't find your home in the forest?"

"Don't be silly. Only another witch could find out where I live. And you're not a witch, are you, darling?"

"No, I'm not," said the woman. "But I do know where you live—at the bottom of a well!"

"How did you know that?" screamed the witch. "A guess, that's all it was! A lucky guess!"

"And would you call this a guess?" asked the woman, opening her pouch and taking out the iron knocker shaped like a scorpion. She threw the iron scorpion to the witch, and the instant it touched the witch's hand, it turned into a real scorpion and bit the witch's finger. The witch screamed loudly and turned into

stone right before the woman's eyes, while the scorpion turned back into iron and fell to the floor.

Without wasting a minute, the woman took the ring off the witch's stone finger. Then she took a hammer and broke the stone witch into a hundred little pieces, and these stones she threw into a sack along with the iron scorpion. She tied the sack as tightly as she could and gave it to her husband and told him to drop it in the deepest well, for that is where the witch liked to live. This he did.

So it was that the woman and her husband and their son lived happily ever after, and no one was ever bothered by the forest witch again.

EASTERN EUROPE: SEVENTEENTH CENTURY

THE TAILORS
AND THE GIANT

Og was a great giant who was saved from the Flood by riding on the roof of Noah's ark. When the waters went down and the ark came to rest, Og wandered around the world for a long, long time. His travels took him everywhere, and that is why stories about him are told in so many lands.

Now Og took such gigantic steps that it did not take him very long to go from the warmth of the south to the cold of the north. And when he arrived in the land of Poland, it was the middle of winter. The truth is that Og was not used to cold

and snow, and he began to shiver. "What I need is a coat," he decided. "I will find a tailor to make me a warm coat."

So on he walked, and after only one giant step he came to a town.

The people of that little town had heard the giant's footsteps when he still was many miles away. "It's an earthquake!" they cried, and they rushed out of their houses. But when they saw that it was an enormous giant, they hurried back inside and hid under their beds.

So when Og came to the town, there was no one to be seen, but Og knew that the people were only hiding. He knocked on the roof of one of the houses with his little finger. "Come out!" he shouted. And the man who lived there rushed out of the house, fearing that the giant would knock it down. "Where does the tailor live?" roared Og. The frightened man could not speak. All he could do was point to a house down the road.

Without another word Og turned away. He reached for the house of the tailor and picked it up in one hand, tailor and all. The tailor was certain that his life was about to come to an end, so he closed his eyes and prayed with all his might.

When he opened his eyes, the tailor saw a giant eye staring at him through one of the windows. "Are you a tailor?" roared a thunderous voice.

"Yes, yes," squeaked the tailor, his knees shaking so hard that they knocked against each other.

"Good!" said Og. "Then you can make me a coat. And hurry up, will you? I'm cold."

The tailor sighed with relief. "It will take a year or more to

make a coat big enough for this giant," he thought. "At least I have another year to live."

But just then he heard the giant's voice again.

"How long will it take before the coat is ready?" Og roared.

"A year," answered the tailor in his small voice.

"What!" shouted Og. "Why, that coat had better be ready in a week, or this whole town will be nothing but dust!"

With that, the angry giant put the tailor's house down and went to huddle in the warmest place he could find. And the tailor dashed out of his house, calling loudly for all the townsfolk to come together. Soon they were all gathered in the synagogue, and the tailor told them of Og's demand. "What shall we do? Oh, what shall we do?" they cried. At last they all agreed to rush off in different directions, to different towns, and tell all the tailors everywhere to come at once, to help sew the coat for the giant Og. For if the giant trampled one town, he could just as well trample another, and so it was clear that they all needed to help each other.

And that is exactly what happened. By the third day there were one hundred tailors all gathered together in the town square. First they had to measure the giant for his new coat. How big was he? What size coat would he need? The task was not an easy one, for when they had put ten tape measures together, they had measured only as high as the giant's knee.

But at last the measuring was done and the tailors sewed away as fast as they could. Each one worked on a large square of the coat, as big as ten blankets, and they worked so hard there was no time for gossip. The scissors snipped and the needles stitched from morning till night.

Soon the week was almost over, and it was time to sew together the sections of the coat. Just then a great cry shook the
room. But it was not the giant—this time it was the littlest tailor.
"Oh no," he shouted, "we have made a terrible mistake!" In their
hurry, the tailors had each sewn a different color cloth. Some
pieces were pink; some were blue. Some had stripes; some had
squares. Some were polka-dotted; some had flowers. It was a
crazy, mixed-up coat indeed, for no two of the sections were the
same.

What could they do? The giant would be coming back for
his coat at any moment. They had to sew it together, even if it
did look like a crazy quilt. So the tailors rushed to fit the
pieces together into a giant coat, and just as they finished the
last sleeve, they heard the thundering steps of the giant.

They looked at the coat. How strange it was, of every color a
person could imagine, with stripes and flowers and polka dots.
Some buttons were on the right side; some were on the left. One
side had a pointed collar; on the other side the collar was round.
What a dreadful mess! Surely the giant would be furious when he
saw that coat! And his footsteps were coming closer and closer!
What could the tailors do?

One after another the frightened tailors jumped into one of
the coat's huge pockets, and the last one to jump inside saw that
the giant was almost there. A moment later they felt the coat rise
high, high up in the air, and they all huddled together inside the
dark pocket. All at once the giant let loose with a roar. The tailors
were certain that he was angry about the mixed-up coat. But they
were wrong. It was a roar of joy. In fact, Og loved his coat, for no

other giant had ever had a coat like this one! Besides, it made him feel much warmer.

All of him, that is, except his hands. His hands were cold. The tailors had not had time to make him gloves. So Og put his hands into his pockets and made fists, because he was so chilled. And when he did, all the tailors were caught up in one fist and were squeezed so hard, they thought they would never take another breath. Their faces became as pale as chalk.

But all of a sudden Og relaxed his grip and sat down. In a few moments the tailors heard the giant snoring, and they realized that Og felt so warm and cozy that he had fallen right to sleep.

Then, as fast as they could, the tailors climbed out of the giant's pocket and ran to their homes. And when they got there, they told everyone about their adventure.

And what did Og do? Why, when he woke up, he decided to return to the south, where it is warm, so that he wouldn't have to keep his hands in his pockets all the time. And that is what he did.

And what did the tailors do? Why, they recovered from their fright. But after that they all had pale faces, every single one of them, for as long as they lived.

POLAND: ORAL TRADITION

THE RABBI
WHO BECAME
A WEREWOLF

Long ago, in the land of Uz, there lived a wise and kind-hearted rabbi. Anyone in need of a Sabbath meal was always welcome at his table. But the rabbi's wife was a stingy woman who hated to part with even a crust of bread. "If you didn't bring home so many students," she would scold, "we would have more to eat ourselves." Her husband paid no mind to her nagging and commanded that everyone who came to the door, especially the poorest of beggars, be given a meal.

Now one year, as Passover approached, the rabbi decided to take twelve of his best students with him into the forest, one for

each of the Twelve Tribes. There they would live for forty days and nights, and spend Passover in the wilderness, as had the children of Israel in the time of Moses.

On the last of the forty days, as the rabbi was washing his hands in a spring, he saw a small weasel running by, with a gold ring in its mouth. Much amazed, he chased the weasel, and when the animal dropped the ring, the rabbi picked it up. He polished it on his coat, and before long the golden ring shone in the sun. That was when he noticed the inscription on the inside. It read: "Not empty, but full."

Someone else might have wondered at this meaning, but not the rabbi, who had spent so many years in the study of secrets and mysteries. "Why, this must be a magic ring," he thought. He decided to test it, so he slipped it on his finger and began to chant a spell that he had once read in a very old book:

"Ring of gold,
Ring of old,
Do my bidding
As you're told:

I wish I had a gold coin for every one of the students who have remained here with me these forty days!" And no sooner had he finished speaking than a leather bag lay at his feet, and inside the bag were gleaming gold coins—twelve in all.

The rabbi returned to his students and gave one gold coin to each and every one. The students were overjoyed, and they made a vow to use the money to build a new school where others could

come to learn. And, indeed, they did build a yeshivah that was the finest in all the land.

But the rabbi's wife was jealous. "Where did the money come from?" she demanded to know. Her husband told her only that God had sent them a miracle.

But the wife kept up her nagging. "Where did the money come from?" she kept asking over and over. "If you just tell me this one thing, I will leave you alone." Still her husband said nothing. So one Sabbath when the rabbi had just lain down for his afternoon nap, she approached him, pretending to weep. "I can't bear it any longer," she cried. "I fear that you have turned into a robber. Where else could the money have come from?" Horrified at her words, the rabbi told the truth about the weasel and the ring and about the wish that had come true.

The wife demanded to see the ring. At first the rabbi refused, but she made it clear that he would get no rest until he showed it to her. So at last the rabbi rose and went into his study, and she followed. And as he took out the ring he had hidden in a drawer, she snatched it from his hand. Oh, she could hardly wait to try it out. "I wish I had a huge house," she said as she clutched the ring tightly. Nothing happened. Then she started to scold. "Husband, what a fool you are! Do you expect me to believe that this worthless ring brought you gold?"

So, to make her stop nagging, the rabbi taught her the magic words. After that she smiled and seemed satisfied, and the rabbi returned to his afternoon nap. But the moment she heard his snoring, his wife crept back into the study, opened the drawer, and pulled out the ring. Then she slipped it on her finger and said:

"Ring of gold,
Ring of old,
Do my bidding
As you're told:

Since my husband likes to live in the wilderness, let him become a werewolf, prowling the forest!"

No sooner were these words spoken than the sleeping rabbi's body vanished, and he awoke to find himself trapped in the body of a wild beast. It was as if he had been pulled out of one body and pushed into another. All at once he was a growling wolf. He bent low and leaped through the window, running off into the woods.

At first the wolf paid no attention to the rabbi inside him. But little by little the rabbi's soul began to influence that of the wolf. In this way many lives were saved. But the villagers still lived in fear, for the werewolf had been seen running through the forest. No one set foot on the street after sundown, and at night the houses were boarded up.

At the yeshivah the students were startled at the rabbi's sudden disappearance. For forty days they waited for his return. And after that, when he still did not come back, they became worried indeed.

The wife too pretended to be worried, and asked them to form a group to search for him. Secretly she thought, "Let them go to the forest. Perhaps a few of them will serve as food for the were-wolf." For the truth is that she cared nothing about the yeshivah, and now that she had gotten rid of the rabbi, she would try to get rid of the students as well. Meanwhile, she turned away every beggar who showed up at her door.

But when the students set out to find the rabbi, they were warned by the villagers to return. No human could remain alive against the power of a werewolf. And so they prayed that wherever the rabbi might be, he was safe from that savage beast.

Meanwhile, the wife began to live a life of luxury. Every day she wished on the ring:

"Ring of gold,
Ring of old,
Do my bidding
As you're told."

At first she asked for a large house, then servants, then furs, then jewels. No one could imagine where her riches had come from.

All this time the rabbi's soul suffered terribly inside the body of the werewolf. In time the rabbi realized that his wife must have stolen the magic ring and brought this curse upon him. He knew that he must somehow obtain the ring, for that was his only hope of turning himself back into a human being. So one night, when there was a full moon, the werewolf came out of the forest and approached the home that he had not seen for so long.

Standing outside the door, the rabbi who had become a werewolf heard the loud snoring of his wife, and he knew that she was sound asleep. He pushed hard against the door, and it began to open, creaking loudly. The rabbi was afraid that his wife would wake up, but though she tossed and turned in her sleep, soon she was snoring loudly once more. Then the werewolf crept into the

house and opened the drawer near her bed, and there he saw the ring that had been the source of his misery. So he picked it up with his teeth and ran off into the forest.

The magic words that rang through the forest that night sounded more like barks and howls, but soon the rabbi was a human again. He gave thanks to God that he no longer had to suffer as a werewolf. Then he picked up the ring and made one last wish on it before tossing it deep into the forest. And at that moment his wife was turned into a she-ass. She kicked off the covers and ran out into the night, braying for all to hear.

The werewolf was never seen again, but the next day the rabbi came wandering back into the village, tired and weak and dazed. He told about being lost in the forest, barely able to find food and shelter. His students took care of him and nursed him back to health. When the rabbi was strong enough, they told him that his wife had disappeared, and that no one knew what had happened to her. They also told of a she-ass that had wandered to that house and had refused to leave, so the students had tied her up with the other animals. When the she-ass saw the rabbi, she began to bray loudly, but the rabbi only smiled to himself.

Before long the rabbi recovered his strength and went back to his work. The yeshivah flourished, until it was known throughout the land. And from that time on everyone, rich and poor, was welcome in the rabbi's home.

EASTERN EUROPE: SIXTEENTH CENTURY

THE PURIM
DYBBUK

It was Purim in the city of Tetuan, in the land of Morocco. This was the time for feasting and making merry and reading the story of Queen Esther. Children could shout and make as much noise as they pleased as they marched from house to house disguised as Queen Esther or the wicked Haman. Grown-ups gathered at the homes of their friends, ate big meals, laughed, and drank lots of wine. And often they played tricks on each other.

That Purim, one group of merrymakers, who were already a little tipsy from drinking too much wine, decided to play a prank on their friends. Without letting anyone see, they poured wine

and sulfur into a frying pan and put it on the fire. At the same time, they snuffed out all the candles. The sulfur flared up in the darkness, making their friends' faces look like the pale faces of ghosts. Everyone gasped. Then, smelling the sulfur, they suddenly realized it was a joke, and they laughed so much they could not stop.

Then Yusef, the little boy of the house, was given the job of emptying the frying pan, which still gave off a terrible stench like that of rotten eggs. He carried the pan outside, where trash was thrown, and emptied it. Little did he know that an invisible spirit named Saadah happened to be passing at that very moment, and the smelly mess from the pan spilled all over her. She was furious, and she jumped up and down in anger. "You can't do that to me, you foolish boy!" she shouted. But, of course, the boy heard nothing, for people can't hear spirits even when the spirits shout.

What did Saadah do? She was so angry that she followed the boy back home. She was still invisible. On the way there, Yusef paused to whistle to the birds that lived in the trees outside his house, and they whistled back. Now the birds saw that Saadah was following him, for birds can see spirits, although people can't. But even though they warned Yusef with their whistles, he did not recognize the warning.

Saadah and the boy entered the house. Yusef's mother offered him a cup of milk and a piece of special Purim cake, shaped like the characters in the Purim story. This was his reward for emptying the pan. Yusef, who had waited all year for this special cake, was delighted and ran out into the courtyard to share a small

piece of the cake with the birds. "Surely," he thought, "they should celebrate Purim too."

That was the moment Saadah had been waiting for. Quickly she turned herself into a long, black hair and jumped into the cup. So when Yusef, who did not notice it, drank the milk, he unknowingly swallowed the hair as well. That is how Saadah came to be inside him and to possess his body.

All at once the boy felt strange and fainted. When he opened his eyes, everyone in the room was standing around him. "What happened? What happened?" they asked. But when the boy opened his mouth to speak, it was not his voice that was heard. Instead it was the rasping voice of Saadah. "Is this the way you treat a spirit who hasn't given you any trouble?" she demanded. "What did I do to deserve having that terrible-smelling stuff dumped all over me?"

Even though it was Purim, everyone knew that this wasn't a joke. The voice was far too frightening for that. The poor boy had been possessed by a dybbuk, a wandering spirit that takes over a person's body. Now she would have to be driven out. But how?

The boy's mother knelt beside him. "Yusef, Yusef," she begged, weeping, "come back to me." Saadah only giggled out loud.

The boy's father shouted, "Spirit, dybbuk, leave my son's body at once!"

But Saadah only announced in her hoarse voice: "I will never leave until you guess my name—and that should take about a hundred years! That's the only way you will get rid of me!" And

she laughed hideously. Everyone was speechless, for how could they find out the dybbuk's name?

The rabbi was called at once, and when he came to the door, the boy turned the other way. The boy didn't want to turn his back on the rabbi, but Saadah made him do it.

"Dybbuk, haven't we met before?" asked the rabbi.

"No, why do you say that?" the boy's lips replied, but it was Saadah's voice that was heard.

"Ah, but we have!" the rabbi answered. "I know you. Isn't your name Ifrit?"

"Ha! Ha!" laughed Saadah. "You're trying to trick me. You don't know my name at all."

"Of course I do," said the rabbi. "Now I remember; your name is Igrat."

"Wrong again!" laughed Saadah. "I'm getting tired of this game. I'll give you just one more guess."

"Very well, then," sighed the rabbi. "I guess I'll have to tell you that your name is Saadah."

Now Saadah was shocked. "How did you know my name? How did you know my name?" she shrieked. And, as quickly as she could, she jumped out of the boy's body and flew out the window.

The boy slumped down, exhausted. When he finally spoke, he spoke in his own voice. "All I did was empty the frying pan," he said, still confused over all that had taken place. Everyone sighed with relief. They knew that the Purim dybbuk was gone.

They turned to the rabbi. "How did you find out the spirit's name?" they asked.

"Ah," said the rabbi, "you see, when I arrived at the house, I heard the birds chirping in the courtyard: 'Saadah, Saadah, Saadah, Saadah.' I knew they must be trying to help their friend Yusef, who always feeds them and plays with them. And so I knew that Saadah must be her name."

So it was that Saadah flew as far as she could from that city. Nor did she ever bother any boy or girl again.

MOROCCO: EIGHTEENTH CENTURY

THE PEDDLER
AND THE SPRITE

Monday was market day in the town of Mogilev, and for Mottke the peddler the day was a long one. There in the market he bought pots, pillows, blankets, and all sorts of household items. Then he packed them in his wagon, so that he could take them to the nearby villages to resell.

That day, as Mottke was leaving the market, he passed a poor merchant who had only one bottle for sale. The bottle was made from dark-colored glass, but otherwise it looked like any other wine bottle, with a cork in the top of it. Taking pity on the man, Mottke bought the bottle and tossed it into his sack.

Mottke left town in late afternoon. He prodded the horse to make it hurry, so that they might reach the nearest village before dark. But along the way he came to a crossroads, and by mistake he took the wrong path.

Mottke drove on. Night fell. The moon was hidden, and at last the peddler realized he could not continue in the darkness. So he stopped the wagon and unhitched the horse. Then he built a fire and wrapped himself in some blankets. He reached into his sack for food and wine, and the bottle he pulled out was the bottle he had bought from the poor man. Mottke pulled out the cork, and suddenly a wind howled around him. The fire flickered and went out. Then he heard a strange cackling in the dark.

That is when Mottke knew there must have been an imp or sprite—or even a demon, heaven forbid—in that bottle, and now it had been set free. Already it had blown the fire out. What would it do next?

Another peddler might have remained speechless and trembling. But not Mottke. He said in a calm voice: "*Shalom Aleichem, imp.*"

"*Aleichem Shalom,*" a strange voice replied.

"What were you doing in that bottle?" the peddler asked.

"Waiting for someone like you to set me free," the imp replied.

"And what kind of imp are you?" Mottke asked.

"A Letz," the voice replied.

Mottke breathed a sigh of relief. A Letz is really more of a sprite, and thus much less dangerous than a demon. It did not in-

tend to do real harm but loved to play pranks. That's what the Letz was famous for, and now that it was free, it was sure to cause trouble wherever it went.

But what could Mottke do, out there in the dark forest? If only he had not opened the bottle! For the Letz could not have come at a worse time, especially since Rosh Hashanah, the New Year, had just passed, and Yom Kippur was soon approaching. This was no time for jokes. But now that the sprite was free, it would surely play all sorts of pranks on the people of the villages.

Mottke struggled to stay awake, but in the middle of the night he just couldn't keep his eyes open any longer. That is when the Letz jumped from behind the tree where it was hiding and hid beneath some sacks in the wagon. So it was that at the very first village where Mottke stopped the next morning, strange things began to happen:

Stones of all sizes fell from the sky! And as if that weren't scary enough, the stones went through the roofs and then the ceilings, passed through the bodies of the people who lived there, and disappeared. "What happened?" people cried. "The stones must be bewitched!" And the Letz—invisible, of course— chuckled to itself.

And in the very next village Mottke visited, every rope turned to sand. Pots that were held up from the ceilings by ropes came crashing down, and everyone was very frightened.

So it went in every village Mottke passed through. Strange events took place that no one could explain, for no one but Mottke realized they were being caused by a Letz.

On Friday morning, Mottke returned to his home in Minsk so that he could spend the Sabbath with his wife and children. The Letz, still hiding in Mottke's wagon, rode to town as well.

That very evening, when the rabbi of Minsk recited the blessing over the wine and sipped a bit from the kiddush cup, he made an awful face. The wine had turned to vinegar! So too did the wine in every other household in Minsk. People worried, whispering in fright. And the Letz? It laughed so hard that its belly shook.

Thus a few days passed. The Letz kept up its tricks. Every time people tried to cross over the city's bridge, a wind rose up and blew off their hats and scarfs. Even the city's animals were victims of the Letz. One morning a cat that lived outside the rabbi's house playfully pushed a mouse it had just caught. But— *poof!*—the mouse disappeared. The cat blinked. It looked around. Where could the mouse have gone? And then, as suddenly as it had vanished, the little mouse appeared again across the room, taunting the cat.

Other strange things began to happen. All the milk in town went sour, even milk fresh from the cow. And almost every night the fire went out in every stove, even though there was plenty of wood to keep it burning. People were very worried, for it was almost Yom Kippur. But the Letz enjoyed every single bit of mischief and only giggled harder to itself.

But on the day of Yom Kippur, when all the townsfolk went to synagogue to pray, the Letz was in a bad mood. There was not a crumb to be found in any of the Jewish houses, nor a drop of water in a glass or cup, for Yom Kippur is a day of fasting. By

afternoon the sprite began to grow weak. And then, to make matters even worse, when the sun went down, there came a piercing, high-pitched blast that echoed through the streets and was made even louder by the stillness around it. It was the sound of the shofar, a ram's horn, being blown on Yom Kippur. The Letz clasped its hands over its ears. But the sound went on and on. The Letz had to hide, but where?

Remembering the peddler's soft sack, the sprite made its way at once to Mottke's wagon. It shoved pillows and blankets around to make a bed, jumped into the sack, and fell asleep.

The next morning, when Mottke saw the mess in his wagon, he knew at once what had happened. And when he saw the strange lump in his sack, Mottke guessed that the Letz was still there. He dared not look inside for fear that the sprite would escape, so he quickly tied the top end of the sack into a strong knot and drove his wagon out of town.

The peddler drove for a long distance, because he wanted to take the Letz as far from Minsk as possible. And all the time that he was driving, the sprite was sound asleep, for it still had not recovered from the shock of hearing the shofar. But when the wagon hit a large rock, the jolt awakened the Letz. And when it tried to get out of the sack, it found that it could not. Then it listened and heard the peddler singing to himself:

"The Letz will soon be gone,
The Letz will soon be gone,
I'll drop it down the deepest well,
The Letz will soon be gone."

Now when the Letz heard this, it was terrified, and it jumped right out of the wagon, sack and all. The startled peddler saw the sack running down the road into the forest, but surprised as he was, he couldn't help laughing. Soon the sack disappeared into the forest, and though Mottke was sorry that he didn't have the chance to drop it down a well, he was glad to be rid of the sprite once and for all. "Good riddance, Mr. Letz!" he called out loud.

And what happened to the sprite? No one knows for sure, but there were reports of folks who had seen a sack running through the forest. Perhaps the Letz is still in the sack to this very day, waiting for someone to release it. Or perhaps it made its way out and went to play pranks in a different town. What we know for sure is that Mottke the peddler, and the people of Minsk, never saw it again.

EASTERN EUROPE: ORAL TRADITION

SOURCES AND COMMENTARY

The study of Jewish folklore has been immeasurably assisted by the creation of the Israel Folktale Archives (IFA), under the directorship of Professors Dov Noy of The Hebrew University and Aliza Shenhar of The University of Haifa. Our grateful thanks are due to Professors Noy and Shenhar, and to Edna Hechal, curator of the archives, for access to the rich material of the IFA. We would also like to thank Toni Markiet, our editor at HarperCollins, for her valuable suggestions and support. We also wish to gratefully acknowledge the assistance of Arielle North Olson in the editing of these stories.

Each of the tales included has been grouped according to the Aarne-Thompson (AT) system, found in *The Types of the Folktale* by Antti Aarne, translated and enlarged by Stith Thompson (Helsinki: 1961). Specific Jewish additions to these types are listed according to the type index of Heda Jason, found in *Fabula*, volume 7, pp. 115–224 (Berlin: 1965) and in *Types of Oral Tales in Israel: Part 2* (Jerusalem: 1975). Reference to these tale types will be of use to those seeking both Jewish and non-Jewish variants of the tales included in this collection.

Refer to the editors' previous collections of Jewish folklore for other examples of Jewish fairy tales, especially *Elijah's Violin & Other Jewish Fairy Tales*, edited by Howard Schwartz (Oxford University Press, 1994), and *The Diamond Tree: Jewish Tales from Around the World*, edited by Howard Schwartz and Barbara Rush (HarperCollins, 1991).

THE WONDER CHILD (Egypt)

IFA 6405. Collected by Ilana Zohar from her mother, Flora Cohen. AT 412: The Maiden With a Separable Soul in a Necklace. A variant is IFA 4859, told by Esther Mikhael of Iraqi Kurdistan to her granddaughter, Esther.

The fact that the wonder child is born with her soul in a jewel indicates the miraculous nature of her birth. The theme of a magical glowing jewel is a popular one in Jewish folklore. Noah was said to have hung such a glowing jewel in the ark, illuminating it for the forty days and nights of the Flood. So too was Abraham said to have worn such a jewel, which healed anyone who peered into it. "The Wonder Child" is an Egyptian variant of Grimms' "Snow White," with elements of Perrault's "Sleeping Beauty."

THE LONG HAIR OF THE PRINCESS (Libya)

IFA 6057, collected by Zalman Baharav from David Hadad of Libya. AT 653: The Four Skillful Brothers, and AT 301A: Quest for a Vanished Princess.

This tale of the combined efforts of seven men to save the

princess held prisoner in a palace at the bottom of the sea is characteristic of a popular tale type found in North African Jewish folklore. Such tales often present the reader with a dilemma at the end, such as that found here about which one of the young men most deserves to marry the princess. Before revealing her choice, those reading or telling this tale to children might want to ask for their opinion about which one the princess should wed. For another example of this type of tale, see "The Mute Princess" in *Elijah's Violin & Other Jewish Fairy Tales*.

THE BLACK CAT (Morocco)

IFA 8902, collected by Devorah Dadon-Wilk from her mother, Hefziba Dadon. AT 476*-* A: Midwife to Demons.

Midwives have served as heroines in Jewish tales ever since Puah and Shifrah in the Book of Exodus (Ex. 1:15–21). This tale of a midwife who goes to the realm of the demons in order to assist in a birth is found in many versions in the Israel Folktale Archives. It is also one of the best examples of a women's tale—that is, a tale told by women to other women in order to present positive feminine role models and examples of how young girls should behave in dangerous situations. Grandmother's statement that "Just doing a good deed is my reward" is a Jewish ethical principle found in *Pirke Avot*, one of the tractates of the Talmud. For a Kurdish version of this tale, see "The Reward of a Midwife" in *The Jews of Kurdistan*, edited by Baruch Rand and Barbara Rush (Toledo Board of Jewish Education and the American Association for Jewish Education, 1978). For a Czech variant, see "The Underwater Palace" in *Lilith's Cave: Jewish Tales of the Supernatural*, edited by Howard Schwartz (Oxford University Press, 1991).

THE FOREST WITCH (Eastern Europe)

From *Nifla'ot ha-Tzaddikim* (Hebrew) (Piotrkow: 1911). AT 500: The Name of the Helper.

This tale is found in many versions in both Eastern European and Middle Eastern Jewish folklore. It is a warning tale about the dangers of making light of wedding vows, which Jewish law requires be fulfilled even if they are made in jest. For variants of this tale, see "The Finger" and "The Demon in the Tree" in *Lilith's Cave*. The determined search by the bride in "The Forest Witch" for the home of the witch makes this a variant of "Rumpelstiltskin" from *Grimms' Fairy Tales*.

THE TAILORS AND THE GIANT (Eastern Europe)

IFA 7249. Collected by Samuel Zanvel Pipe from his family. From *Sippure Am Mi'Sanok* (Hebrew), collected by Samuel Zanvel Pipe, edited by Dov Noy (Haifa: 1967). AT *1854: Jokes on Tailors. A variant is IFA 3741, collected by Moshe Vigisser from Menachem Urali of Russia.

Og, the biblical giant, is the primary giant found in Jewish folklore. Here he wanders into Eastern Europe in the winter and demands that a coat be made for him. This tale humorously explains why tailors have pale faces. See "The Giant Og and the Ark" in *The Diamond Tree* for the tale about how Og was saved from the Flood by riding on Noah's ark.

THE RABBI WHO BECAME A WEREWOLF (Eastern Europe)

From *Maaseh Buch* (Yiddish) (Basel: 1602). AT 555: The Fisher and His Wife, and AT 560: The Magic Ring.

This is the most famous werewolf tale in all of Jewish folklore. It is also a Jewish variant of "The Fisherman and His Wife" from *Grimms' Fairy Tales*. For another werewolf tale, see "The Boy Israel and the Werewolf" in *Lilith's Cave*.

THE PURIM DYBBUK (Morocco)

From *Neshamat Haim* 120a (Hebrew), edited by Rabbi Menasche ben Yisroel (Amsterdam: 1752). AT 500: The Name of the Helper, and AT 1168: Ways of Expelling Devils.

A dybbuk is an evil spirit that takes possession of a living person. Tales about dybbuks became prominent in Jewish lore in the sixteenth century in both Palestine and Eastern Europe. Here the possession occurs because the boy empties the contents of a frying pan onto the invisible spirit, who immediately takes revenge. As is customary in all dybbuk tales, it is a wise rabbi who finds a way to exorcise the dybbuk. This story also shows how people of that time celebrated Purim: eating cakes shaped like Purim characters, dressing up as characters in the story, merrymaking in the streets, and having parties at home.

THE PEDDLER AND THE SPRITE (Eastern Europe)

Collected by Shlomo Vinner from Yehuda Yaari. AT 331: The Spirit in a Bottle, and AT 1635*: Eulenspiegel's Tricks.

Jewish folklore tells of many types of demons and imps, who have varying degrees of evil powers and intents. The sprite in this tale is a Letz, a uniquely Jewish imp or hobgoblin often found in Eastern

European folklore, who is more likely to play tricks on people than to harm them. This is characteristic of the types of tales told by merchants, who entertained each other by recounting fantastic tales.

GLOSSARY

(All of the following terms are Hebrew unless noted.)

Bar Mitzvah   The ceremony at which a Jewish boy of thirteen becomes an adult.

Dybbuk   A spirit that possesses a living person and must be exorcised.

Kiddush Cup   The cup used to perform the blessing over wine.

Letz   (Yiddish) A mischievous sprite popular in Yiddish folklore.

Purim   A Jewish festival celebrating the story told in the Book of Esther.

Rosh Hashanah   The Jewish New Year.

Shalom Aleichem   A greeting spoken by Jews upon meeting each other. Literally, "Peace unto you." The reply, *Aleichem Shalom*, means "Unto you, peace."

Shammes	(Yiddish) The person in charge of taking care of the synagogue.
Shavuoth	A Jewish harvest festival, which is also celebrated as the day of the Giving of the Torah at Mount Sinai.
Shofar	The ram's horn that is ritually blown on Rosh Hashanah and Yom Kippur.
Talmud	The most sacred Jewish text after the Bible, codified in the fifth century.
Yeshivah	A school for talmudic and rabbinic studies.
Yom Kippur	The Day of Judgment, on which God decides a person's fate for the coming year. A day of fasting and prayer.

THE WONDER CHILD